THE RETURN

Doc Beck Westerns Book 9

SARAH ELISABETH SAWYER

THE RETURN
The Return © 2023 by Sarah Elisabeth Sawyer
All rights reserved.

RockHaven Publishing
P.O. Box 1103
Canton, Texas 75103

Editor: Lynda Kay Sawyer
Cover Design: Mollie E. Reeder
Author Photo by R. A. Whiteside. Courtesy of the National Museum of the American Indian, Smithsonian Institution

Print ISBN: 978-1-956043-11-2

PROLOGUE

The line at the train station was inordinately long, but Roger Graham would have waited until hell froze over to buy a ticket to Omaha, Nebraska.

The line moved forward in the cavernous St. Louis Union Station.

Graham pressed closer to the ticket window. Four more people to go until he could purchase a ticket that would take him to confront the infamous "Doc Beck" before she set one foot on the Omaha Indian Reservation. At least, that was Graham's dream.

His ill mother, who he was visiting in St. Louis, would prevent that extraordinary moment of looking Rebekah LaRoche in the eye and telling her he was working to have her blackballed with every state medical board. She would have her medical license revoked in the states of Nebraska, Wyoming, and anywhere she wanted to light. If she tried to practice medicine anywhere, he'd see her fined or jailed.

The line moved forward. Three to go.

When Graham read the article calling LaRoche a sophisticated spitfire and heroine of the west, it infuriated him. Women doctors like her, an Indian woman no less, had no business holding human lives in her hands. He knew that better than anyone.

Two to go.

Graham was the only man who knew the truth and he would be the one to stop her. One way or another. He must make sure she caused no more harm as a physician. As Lt. Governor of Missouri, he no longer just had friends in high places. He was in high places.

One to go.

He should not have let her depart the Omaha Indian Reservation. As the agent there at the time, he could have forced her into a life of destitution and solitude right on the reservation. His intent in banning her was to get her to stop practicing medicine and ensure she didn't rip away the life of a man's wife and daughter ever again.

Now she was returning, sneaking onto the reservation with the help of her brother. Though Graham was no longer the Indian agent on the Omaha Reservation, he kept close tabs on it from his new job in Jefferson City.

When he learned that Amos LaRoche requested permission to leave the reservation for the first time in his life, Graham knew there could be only one reason.

The man at the ticket window in front of Graham was arguing with the clerk about a schedule error he claimed. Graham clenched his fist and pressed it atop his derby hat to hold it in place as a gust blew from an incoming train huffing into the station. He shouldn't be impatient about buying this ticket. It was for tomorrow's train. But the sooner he had it in his pocket, the sooner he would feel peace of mind, knowing he was one step closer to ending Rebekah LaRoche's reckless behavior.

The man finally consented to the printed schedule the clerk showed him. He grumbled, handed over a bill and swiped his ticket from the clerk with a grunt. He moved away from the window, then turned back to spit out one last argument, but Graham was already taking up the space and attention of the clerk.

The young man looked frazzled as he snapped, "May I help you, sir?"

Graham spoke soft, calm. "I need a ticket for tomorrow's train to Omaha, Nebraska."

The young man's features relaxed at his kind tone. Graham had a way of doing that. Putting people at ease when he needed to. It was a way to influence powerful men. It was his key to destroying Rebekah LaRoche.

The clerk stamped a ticket for Omaha and handed it to him as Graham offered the payment. He tucked the ticket in his coat pocket and tipped his hat at the clerk. "Have a good day, son."

The young man stood a little taller. "You have a fine trip, sir."

Graham patted his pocket with the ticket and turned away. He said to himself, "This ticket isn't for me."

CHAPTER 1

Hair still damp from her baptism, Rebekah stood with her back to the stone fireplace behind the desk in Doctor McKinnon's study. She clasped her hands behind her, both to warm them by the low fire and to keep from wringing them as he stood on the opposite side of the room near the front windows.

Doctor Robert T. McKinnon faced away from her, his suit coat laid aside and hands deep in his pockets as he watched the early sunset from the window. It was the stance he took when negotiating to prevent trouble. He was excellent at diffusing tension.

The stance would have worked with Rebekah if it had not been for the deep creases in his forehead and the turned down corners of his lips. If it had not been for the way he abruptly laid aside the letter she had received today. It hovered on his desk between them, a chasm she didn't feel either of them would cross.

The door to the study was closed, but through it, Rebekah heard Jimmy's cackle of laughter from the parlor. Most of the McKinnon ranch hands were hanging around in there. Doctor McKinnon had promised them a feast in the formal dining room after the baptisms, with the caveat that they clean up first from their dip in the lake. It wasn't a hard sale for the cowboys who rushed off to the bunkhouse, Jimmy in tow, though he protested. He wanted to meet the stranger standing on the bank who waited for Rebekah.

Soaked head to toe, Rebekah had urged Jimmy to go with the men as she let Laramie Jones help her out of the water and up the steep bank. Save for Doctor McKinnon, Laramie was the only one who knew who this man was.

Rebekah hadn't realized that Laramie still held her hand until he released it and stepped away, allowing her a private moment with her brother. Amos LaRoche. The coldness left in Laramie's absence chilled her, a foreboding feeling reflected in Amos's eyes.

Her brother stood at the same height as she, his brown-black braids coming from underneath a wide-brimmed felt hat overlapping his button-down shirt. He wore a lightweight brown jacket, hardly sufficient for the coming winter. Rebekah knew that back home on the Omaha Indian Reservation he would embrace buffalo hide robes when the winter turned serious and the mercury dipped to twenty below. They had survived on the plains all their lives, though in different ways.

Rebekah hadn't laid eyes on her brother in three years. He hadn't changed, a mirror of their father in face and form, though not in beliefs. His gaze was as hard as flint.

Amos held a letter out to her, the missive pinched between his thumb and forefinger, leaving most of it exposed for her to grasp. She took it, respectful of the way he did not want her to touch him, still under the condemnation of his disease, as if she wasn't a physician who laid hands on infirm people regularly.

Rebekah unfolded the letter and read it, her heartbeat speeding up. She met Amos' eyes. "Will you stay while I decide?"

"I will come for you tomorrow."

That letter, stained with lake water from her baptism, lay on the desk between Rebekah and Doctor McKinnon now. The words shouted accusations at her, accusations of neglect. The water stains were accusations of the drastically different path she had chosen from her brother. Yet it was the path their father had walked, and the burning inside Rebekah told her that path would lead her to the end of her dreams and years of work. The letter would let her do no less.

Doctor McKinnon turned from the window at last and the look in his eyes let her know he would not bless her decision to return to the Omaha Indian Reservation.

When he remained silent, Rebekah knew it was her burden to speak first. "I'm sorry, Uncle Robert. But I must go."

Her words sounded raw and throaty. If only she would come down with pneumonia! The decision could be put off, could save the pain reflected in Doctor McKinnon's gaze.

Doctor McKinnon slowly shook his head. "You must not."

Another shriek of laughter told her the ranch hands were having too good of a time in the parlor. Laramie Jones would tame them down unless, as Rebekah suspected, he lingered in the foyer near the closed door to Doctor McKinnon's study.

Rebekah could feel the flame of the low fire slowly burning her hands but she couldn't move. "My people are dying. If Susan were well, I would continue to wait. But now she is one of the dying."

Doctor McKinnon slowly shook his head and turned back to the window, his lips pulled into a hard line. "If we return you to the reservation under approval of the current governor and Indian agent, you can remain there for decades to come. If you return now, you destroy what we've tried to accomplish for three...long...years."

The way he dragged out the last few words slammed into Rebekah. He truly cared for her heart's mission.

There were times when she wondered if his having the ability to send her out on medical missions wherever she was needed in the west was something he valued doing more so than her returning to her people. But he felt the pain alongside her, her misery of being separated from her people and from the very reason she had undergone medical training. He had sponsored her and suffered everything with her.

Yet there was still no way he could understand how deep the burns seared into her soul as they did now.

"Be that as it may," Rebekah said, voice a whisper, "I must return. Susan has been one of my dearest friends and lives will be lost without her. Her life is far more valuable than anything I could contribute on this earth."

Doctor McKinnon jerked away from the window so fast it was as if a gunshot had whizzed by him. His hands came out of his pockets and he strode to the desk, picking up the letter and shaking it at Rebekah.

"You are every bit as valued as Susan! Why do you think they've sent for you? You belong with your people and we will have you there within a year. I believe that with all my heart. But if you go now, you will lose everything."

She tried to smile. "I can always come home to the McKinnon Ranch, can't I?"

Doctor McKinnon's face fell, and he tossed the letter back on the desk. Rebekah regretted her light words. Of course she always had a home with Uncle Robert. His words showed how much he understood what *everything* meant to her—her people, her medical practice, and the calling to blend them all her days. Her remark had cheapened that and she stepped toward the desk, her hands burning. She reached out and touched Doctor McKinnon's sleeve.

"Please try to understand. I don't want to hurt you. I don't want to disrespect everything you've done for me. But I must go to Susan. I must...go to my people." Her voice broke and she sucked in a breath to stay the tears.

Doctor McKinnon raised his head. His voice was husky with his own tears.

"If you chase trouble hard enough, it will catch you."

In the echo of his words, she remembered all the warnings he had given her.

Stay out of trouble. Stay out of the papers.

As long as she complied and kept controversy out of her life, she had a chance of receiving government sanction to return and practice medicine on the Omaha Indian Reservation.

But time was up. If trouble was going to catch her, it would catch her doing one last deed for her people.

"I must go."

Doctor McKinnon planted two fists on his desk and hung his head between his shoulders. Rebekah's heart twisted. It shattered when he raised his gaze and met her eyes.

This was perhaps the worst moment of her life.

She'd endured burying two parents, the rejection of her brother, the banishment from her people, terrors in the wild West. All those things were life circumstances that happened to her. This time, she was choosing to intentionally hurt one of the people she loved and respected her entire life. Someone who had only done her good all her life.

Unable to bear up under his agonized gaze, Rebekah snatched the letter and hurried around the desk to the door. Flinging it open, she saw her path to the stairwell wasn't clear.

Laramie stood by the banister, one arm propped on it as he leaned to the side, staring out the window by the front door. His attention came to her immediately, oblivious of the ruckus in the parlor behind him.

Rebekah couldn't hold his gaze. She hurried toward the stairs, hoping he would let her by, but knowing better. He took a half step to halt her flight up the stairs, one hand spread open toward her.

"When do you leave?"

His voice was soft, his words surprising. He didn't know what was in the letter, but he didn't need to. He'd seen her brother and knew she was being summoned home.

He also believed she shouldn't go, same as Doctor McKinnon. But he also knew she would go.

"Tomorrow," the single word slipped out. Somehow, that one word tasted like *forever* on her tongue.

CHAPTER 2

There was no leaving the ranch before anyone stirred the next morning, so Rebekah took her time, packing her carpetbag and medical bag for her trip home.

She touched the framed photograph she kept of her father and stepmother by her bedside. She would leave it there at McKinnon Ranch, the safest place for it. It was the safest place for her as well. But she couldn't stay.

With one last look around the bedroom she had called her own since spending summers there during childhood, Rebekah closed the door quietly. She made her way to the stairs in the weak dawn light. The smell of breakfast coming from the kitchen turned her stomach. She couldn't bear another argument with her uncle before she left.

Rebekah headed straight for the front door. She half expected Doctor McKinnon to be waiting for her on the porch to try and prevent her from leaving.

Instead, she found two unexpected figures on the porch. Sitting side-by-side in the rocking chairs were her brother and Jimmy.

She should have expected Amos there and ready to go. Jimmy too, to see her off. What made her frown were the saddlebags resting in Jimmy's lap. *His* saddlebags.

She put an admonishing hand on her hip, uncertain whether she should scold him teasingly or give him serious doctor orders. She settled on the latter.

"You are to remain in bed for another three days, young man. Especially after the exertion yesterday."

Jimmy popped to his feet, though she didn't miss the way he stayed bent slightly at the waist, nurturing the healing wound in his gut. He slung his saddlebags over his shoulder and grinned. "Ma'am, that baptism did some mighty healing on me. I'm raring and ready to go. Mr. Laramie wants me to escort you there and back, and I always do what the boss man says."

Rebekah squinted in suspicion. Whatever had possessed Laramie to think Jimmy was well enough to travel twenty-seven hours by train and look after her on the reservation?

By all rights and logic, it should be Laramie making the trip back to the reservation with her. He was no more welcome than she, which would make it fitting. But also far too troublesome, and they both knew it.

Jimmy would follow along after her, even if she tried to force him to stay. Laramie knew that, too. He always seemed to know the right path ahead of her.

Amos, a silent cough shaking his shoulders, stood, putting himself between her and Jimmy. He was close, closer than he'd been in so long. But Rebekah felt the chasm between them as their eyes met. His were so distant. Yet he was there to fetch her home. It was enough for Rebekah to gather her fortitude and nod.

"Let's be on our way then."

Steve Bowers drove them into town in Doctor McKinnon's buggy. He said a quiet goodbye to the odd trio as they waited to board the eastbound train in the early afternoon.

Within minutes of the train's departure, Jimmy was fast asleep on the seat next to Rebekah, hat over his eyes, stretched out with his long legs crossed at the ankles, barely out of the aisle. Amos sat across from her, watching the people on the train, though his head never moved.

Carefully, so as not to wake Jimmy, Rebekah reached down to undo the straps on her medical bag. She withdrew the letter from Susan's sister, Rosalie, lifted it to her nose, inhaling the faint scent of prairie and woodsmoke, a sweet aroma of her birthplace. Her fingers trembled just as they had the first time she read the letter.

Dearest Rebekah,

How greatly we have missed you. I am writing now in a desperate plea. It grieves me to pen these words, but Susan is so ill. More than once, we feared she would not survive the summer, sometimes not even the night. She has worked herself to exhaustion. We have nearly given up all hope for her.

If God chooses to take Susan from us, we will accept it. But dear Rebekah, you are a healer like her and how we have longed for your touch for her.

We are so desperate here, we are willing to ask you to do everything within your power to return home. We know the legal challenges—we all faced regulations and denials as we pursued education and careers—but we know God will find a way, if you are willing. That is what my letter is pleading for—that you would be willing. Our prayer is that God will make a way.

Please consider returning to the reservation for your people—and for Susan—as soon as you can.

With my love and respect,
Rosalie

Reading the letter again soothed Rebekah's heart even as it brought tears to her eyes. She was on the right path, despite Doctor McKinnon's disappointment. This letter left her no choice.

She leaned over to tuck the letter closer to the bottom of her medical bag where she wouldn't lose it. Her fingertips brushed another slip of paper. She pulled it out, frowning. Where had this come from?

It only took a moment to recognize Laramie's handwriting. It was short, typical of him. As was being able to slip it into her bag without her knowing. Western men were quite clever at times.

You got to follow the work God leads you to. Just be sure He's leading you.

For all her confidence, Rebekah's courage fled. Was she really following the path God laid for her return to the reservation? Or was she making her own path as she had so often in the past?

Across from her, Amos was unable to suppress a vicious cough. She had her answer. Right or wrong, her path was set.

Rebekah sensed the moment they crossed the state line between Wyoming and Nebraska. She sensed it in the subtle landscape changes that had occurred over the last several miles. She sensed it in the way Amos shifted his shoulders to stare out the window. He had so infrequently left the reservation in his life; he knew the moment as well as she that they were entering the homelands of the Umoho people.

State boundaries hadn't meant a thing to their people for thousands of years. Those of her generation knew only the reservation boundaries and limits prescribed to their people. Ironically, being dismissed from the reservation set Rebekah free to live in the world of her French ancestors, rather than her Omaha ones. Yet she had felt so lost in the wide expanse of the west. This was her anchor. The homeland of her people.

SLEEPING on the train was a miserable experience, but Rebekah worked the stiffness from her neck as the sun rose over the Nebraskan plains. They were coming oh so close to the Omaha and she could feel the spirit of her ancestors waving a greeting through the high grasses outside the train window.

Jimmy, still stretched out nearly into the aisle, broke the essence of the moment when he spoke quietly from beneath his Stetson hat. "Ma'am, you know that fella sitting a couple of rows back? The one that boarded at Columbus?"

Jolted, Rebekah shifted in her seat to look at Jimmy beside her. She had thought he was still asleep from the night as Amos was. The fact that he was so aware of his surroundings reminded her how blessed she was to have him as a friend, even though she wished he were back on the ranch.

She continued turning her head slightly to see who Jimmy was talking about. The seats immediately behind her were empty. But beyond them, a man in a three-piece suit and derby hat was situated on a bench seat, facing her little entourage. He held a newspaper spread open before his face, obscuring most of it. Even so, she was certain she didn't know him.

Facing forward again, she softly asked Jimmy, "What about him?"

Jimmy didn't move his Stetson away from his face. Anyone on the train car would think he was sound asleep. He spoke for her ears only.

"He walked awful slow when he got on the train. And that St. Louis newspaper he's reading is pretty used up, like he's been carrying it around longer than it would take to read it."

Jimmy thumbed up the brim of his hat, showing his sky-blue eyes. He didn't turn his head.

"I don't know, ma'am. You just get a feeling about things sometimes. Know what I mean?"

Rebekah did. She didn't recognize the man, but she could feel his gaze on the back of her neck now. Was that because of Jimmy's suspicion or her paranoia? Why would anyone be following them?

Unfortunately, the answer to that question came with a list of possibilities. She recalled the recent incident of the Medicine Bow Mountains, when Calvin Blackthorn tried to exact revenge on her for his brother's legs. As a doctor in the west, she made more friends than enemies, but she also encountered unusual situations. There was that chance there were more out there like him.

And there was Roger Graham, though it didn't seem possible he would know so quickly that she was traveling back to the reservation. If he did know, would he have sent someone to intercept her?

That possibility made her stomach go cold, and she placed her hand over it to warm it. Across the seat from her, Amos had awakened but not taken an interest in her and Jimmy's quiet conversation. He looked at her now, and Rebekah cut her eyes to one side, hoping he caught sight of the man she indicated behind her. Amos' eyes shifted. They landed for a moment before he resumed looking out the window.

Amos didn't recognize the man either, which meant it was unlikely the new agent from the reservation or any other white man from there.

Who was he then? A figment of Jimmy's adventurous imagination? A manifestation of her greatest fear?

Rebekah hoped to never find out.

She wouldn't take any chances, though. They would not transfer at the junction to go to Wisner, her typical departing point when she left the reservation. It was only twenty miles from there to Logan Creek where Susan lived, but that was too close for comfort.

They would continue on to circle north of the reservation and go all the way to Sioux City. That would double the distance they needed to travel by buggy, but the city was large enough for them to slip away from that man if he was following them. Or anyone else who might want to stop Doc Beck from returning to her people.

CHAPTER 3

The train whistled long and mournful. At least it sounded so to Rebekah's ears as they chugged slowly into the depot at Sioux City. She had scarcely taken her eyes from the train window for the past hour. Rolls of farmland mile after blessed mile had filled her being and her heart. She was home. Truly, truly home!

Jimmy shifted on the bench seat beside her, causing a draft in the space between them. A chill went through her being. That man was still watching them.

The rolling hills gave way to the country metropolis of Sioux City and the up-close view of the train depot startled her after watching the miles stretch so long and far to the horizon.

It was time to get off.

The ever-intuitive Jimmy had the same thought. He used the momentum of the train car jerking to a halt to lean forward, dropping his boots to the floor and sitting up straight. He lifted his hat off his head with a big yawn, raking his fingers through his shaggy blonde hair and turning his head slightly. Rebekah wouldn't have noticed except for the angle he held his hat. He was checking on their spy a few rows back.

Mid-stretch, Jimmy winced and hunched over, dropping his hat back on his head. Rebekah put a hand on his arm, gently pushing his shoulder back so she could face him squarely. She scanned him from his pained expression down to the way his right hand covered his gut.

"Dear Jimmy, I wish you hadn't come."

He squinted his eyes and cocked one eyebrow at her. "You sure about that, ma'am?"

On the seat across from them, Amos hadn't moved, and Rebekah knew he was waiting for the rush of exiting passengers to clear the aisle before trying to get off. The problem was the hole would fill just as quickly with people pressing onto the passenger car. Sioux City was an intersection of humanity.

Rebekah stood slow, sore from the long ride. She took advantage of her modest stretching to glance back at the man a few rows back. He had disappeared.

Perhaps he *was* simply a manifestation of her fears.

Jimmy gathered his saddlebags and her medical bag. It wouldn't do a bit of good to insist he not try to carry anything beyond himself. What did surprise her though, was how quickly Amos came to his feet and stripped the saddlebags from Jimmy's shoulders and snagged the medical bag from him. Without a word, Amos slung the bags over his own shoulder, retrieved Rebekah's carpetbag from the overhead rack, and forged ahead into the oncoming flow of people boarding the train.

Rebekah was surprised Amos was willing to carry her medical bag. It was a symbol of her leaving behind so many of their traditional ways and embracing so many ways of the whites. It represented all Amos despised despite how Rebekah, like her friend Susan, continued to employ their peoples' time-tested remedies and knowledge with their patients.

Jimmy, hand returning to his stomach, offered his other arm to Rebekah. She took it with a firm grip, wanting to make sure he didn't take a tumble as they exited the train.

On the platform, Rebekah froze, halting Jimmy as she took in the sights and sounds of a town she hadn't seen in years.

Growing up on the Omaha Indian Reservation, she was restricted from leaving without permission of the Indian agent. Her father, fluent in English and a practicing Christian, rarely left the reservation. He did insist that his children find their way in the white man's world. He felt it was the only way for them to preserve their family and their people.

One of his children had followed that path. One had not.

Jimmy wiggled his arm that she still grasped. She turned to him with a weak smile.

He inclined his head toward the edge of the platform and the steps leading down from it. "Best catch up with your brother, Miss Rebekah, or he'll be clean out to the reservation without us."

Indeed, Amos was already down the steps and striding up the main street, headed toward the livery stables.

Rebekah used her free hand, reticule dangling by its string, to lift her skirts and hurry across the platform, mindful of her pace for Jimmy. He didn't show any discomfort other than a slight grimace as they lumbered down the stairs and caught up with Amos' long, purposeful strides.

"Amos!"

Rebekah licked her lips, swallowed hard at the taste of his name on her tongue. She hadn't spoken his Christian name for many years. He had not used hers either, not even when he found her at Uncle Robert's ranch. They were not accustomed to calling one another by name, much less by the Christian names their father had given them. Amos had adopted an Omaha name, White Swan, in his teens, though their father refused to use it. Rebekah had found it easier to not address him by name rather than be caught between the two of them once again.

Her brother halted but didn't turn around. Rebekah and Jimmy caught up with him in front of the milliner shop. It caused

Rebekah to recall the first store-bought dress her father bought for her at the milliner in Wisner. She remembered that trip well as a gangly 14 year old who wouldn't be returning to the reservation that day. Not for months because she was headed to school in Elizabeth, New Jersey, along with Susan and her sister Marguerite. She well remembered something the milliner said. *"You're like your father. More white than Omaha."*

Rebekah shook away those thoughts then realized she was shaking her head. She spoke to Amos. "It's getting late in the day, and we don't want to barge in on Susan in the middle of the night. Let's stay at a hotel here and get an early start in the morning."

She could tell Amos did not like her suggestion. He had most likely never stayed one night under a roof owned by white people. Even when he came for her at the ranch, Amos had camped out in the foothills while awaiting her response to return to the reservation.

He did not want to stay in a hotel room.

Before she could think of what to say to convince him, Jimmy pulled away. She glanced at him, her gaze landing on a man across the busy street. He held the same newspaper half covering his face and his eyes dropped to something on the right-hand page. But not before he made the briefest eye contact with Rebekah.

Why was that man watching them?

Would he follow her out to the reservation? Was he waiting for her to cross the boundary line so he could arrest her?

No. She wouldn't be arrested for entering the reservation without permission. She was still an Omaha citizen. But he could report her activity there and all Uncle Robert warned her about would come true.

Rebekah turned back to Amos who stood stock still and straight under the load of Jimmy's saddlebags, her medical bag, and carpetbag. He was accustomed to carrying the burdens of others, but so rarely hers. His shoulders shook with another suppressed cough.

Though traffic on the main street swallowed anything other than a shout, Rebekah kept her voice low. "Brother, I believe that man is following us. You know my enemy and if he somehow learned in advance of my return, it's possible he's sent someone to spy on us. We must be wise. Please."

Amos didn't break from her gaze, didn't move. Rebekah took that as agreement.

Grasping Jimmy's arm again, Rebekah steered him across the street, diagonally from where the tail man was. She needed a solid plan and fast.

Amos following, Rebekah led the way to the Enterprise hotel, taking her time entering and relieved to find a line at the desk. Other passengers from the train had gone straight to the hotel and the line was five people deep. It took several minutes before they were next in line at the desk. An idea was forming in her mind.

Rebekah released Jimmy's arm and withdrew a handkerchief from her reticule to blow her nose, awkward and silly. Partially hidden by Amos, standing behind her, Rebekah scanned the lobby. There were few occupants and none of them was the mystery man. If only he would sneak in before she reached the desk. But her turn had come.

With a sigh, Rebekah replaced her handkerchief and stepped up to the desk. "We would like—"

Behind her, the hotel door clicked open and then closed, almost imperceptibly. Why would someone bother trying to quietly close the door of a hotel lobby?

Realizing the bored clerk was staring at her, Rebekah spoke in an above normal tone, hoping she didn't sound obviously loud. "We would like two rooms, please. And could you place them far apart, on separate floors if you can? My sweet friend here snores terribly."

Jimmy turned to her, lips pulled down in a deep frown. She

tightened her own lips to keep from giggling. Jimmy did snore, though she had exaggerated. She hoped the tail man heard her.

The clerk took down their names and handed off keys—rooms on separate floors—and Rebekah led her little party to the bottom of the stairs. Turning to face Jimmy and Amos gave her a clear view of the hotel lobby. Most of all, the man seated on the settee near the window, newspaper obscuring his face.

Knowing they were too far away for the man to hear, Rebekah spoke in her normally soft tone. "Why don't we meet in the hotel restaurant for dinner in an hour?" She gestured to her right, where a large opening led into the dining area already filled with patrons.

Jimmy lowered his voice. "We need to talk, Miss Rebekah. About that man."

She nodded. "Dinner will be a sufficient time."

Lifting her skirts, she led the way up the stairs and down the hall to her room. Amos' and Jimmy's was one floor up. She unlocked the door and Amos deposited the bags inside without entering. He knew it would be unseemly for a man to enter a woman's room when gossiping guests didn't know they were siblings.

Rebekah turned her attention to Jimmy. "I want you to lie down until dinner. You look as if a herd of longhorns stampeded over you."

Jimmy grinned, his face lightened with relief. "Aw, come on, Miss Rebekah, you know I'm doing just fine. I've got the best doctor in the west tending me."

"And that doctor is ordering you to bed. I'll see...you shortly."

She faltered, wanting to include Amos, but her brother had already headed for the stairs up to the next floor.

Suddenly, Rebekah began trembling all over, as though she were breaking apart from the inside out.

As much as she wanted to return to her people, she wanted her brother back more. It was something she had longed for since she was 14 years old.

Her shoulders shook and she feared wracking sobs would ruin everything she needed to do in her life.

Jimmy gripped her by the shoulders, bringing her head up to meet his eyes. He bent his knees to look straight at her. "Ma'am, you all right?"

Rebekah reached up and squeezed one of his hands. He enveloped her in a fierce hug. He usually had the strangest, sweetest things to say, but right now, his silence was what she needed.

Rebekah wrapped her arms around him, giving him a strong hug to let him know she would be all right and how terribly glad she was that he was alive and that he was there with her.

She released him and he took a step back, hands on her shoulders again. She wasn't sure if she needed the support or he did. She squeezed his wrists and mustered a smile.

"All right, Just Jimmy, you follow doctor's orders now. I'll see you in the dining room soon."

❧

THE DINING ROOM was only half full when Rebekah requested a corner table. She seated herself facing the wall and indicated Jimmy take the seat across from her where he could see the entire room. To her disappointment—or maybe relief—Amos chose not to take dinner with them.

Jimmy and Rebekah maintained a normal conversation throughout dinner, talking about the ranch and the wide-open spaces of the west. Rebekah asked Jimmy if he wanted dessert to which he laughed. Rebekah ordered them two slices of apple pie.

With Jimmy still chuckling, Rebekah asked quietly, "Is he here?"

Still grinning, Jimmy nodded. "He changed his clothes, but it's him all right. He's got a table right next to the door. Who you reckon he is, ma'am?"

Relieved that the man was far enough away to not hear their conversation, Rebekah relaxed her shoulders and continued her casual chitchat manner. "It doesn't seem possible that Roger Graham would have had time to send someone to follow me, but he is a determined man. I do not want that spy, if that's what he is, to follow me to the reservation."

Jimmy nodded, sitting back as the waitress set his pie in front of him, a second one for Rebekah. After she left, Jimmy said, "I'd say he's a professional, but he ain't perfect. I can keep him busy here in town while you skedaddle on out to see your friend."

Rebekah frowned. "I do not like the idea of leaving you on your own."

Jimmy grinned, eyes down as he took his last bite of pie. It always amazed Rebekah how quickly he could shovel in food. "Ma'am, I've been on my own pert near all my life. The good Lord looks out for me."

Rebekah knew that to be quite true. "Well then." She slid her slice of pie over to him. "All we need is a plan."

CHAPTER 4

Rebekah inserted the key to Jimmy and Amos's room, uncertain if she should be sneaky or pretend it was her room. She settled on getting inside as quickly as she could, managing not to fumble her carpetbag and medical bag as she locked the door behind her.

The room was dark. Empty. Where was Amos? Again, she was partly relieved, partly disappointed, but partly frustrated. Amos needed to know of the details of the scheme Jimmy and Rebekah had worked out.

Now, for all she knew, Amos may have decided to go outside of town to camp out. But his bedroll was neatly placed on one of two beds. He would be back. But when?

Rebekah could not wait all night to find out.

Even now, Jimmy was tailing the tail man. When she and Jimmy parted ways at the dining room door, Rebekah had announced her intention to retire for the evening and Jimmy said he would take care of sending a telegram to Doctor McKinnon and let him know they would remain in Sioux City a few days to gather supplies for the reservation before going out there.

All things they wanted the tail man to hear.

Once Jimmy assured her the man was in his room, which Jimmy had learned was right across from hers, she and Amos would sneak out and head straight for the reservation. They would arrive before dawn then travel to Susan's near Macy where Rebekah would do everything she could before the man caught up with her.

When Rebekah asked Jimmy how he knew the man's room number, he confessed he'd distracted the front desk clerk and peeked at the register before meeting her in the dining room. She truly was grateful to have him on this venture.

Now if only Amos would be as cooperative, and kindly come back to the hotel room she rented for him. If he did not, she would leave without him.

That seems to be a mutual habit between them.

She might as well rest. It was going to be a long night.

Sometime later, Rebekah jolted upright. She had fallen asleep across Amos' bed and was now aware of a presence in the room. She reached beneath her medical bag where she had stowed her pepperbox pistol. She had just gripped the handle when a match struck, lighting the darkness and Jimmy's face as he leaned over her.

"Don't shoot, ma'am, it's me. Time to move."

Rebekah pushed herself off the bed. "Do you know where Amos is?" She retrieved her medical bag, slipping the pepperbox inside. Jimmy grabbed her carpetbag and the bed roll.

In the dark, she sensed his discomfort from bending rather than saw it. But there wasn't a trace of it in his voice when he answered.

"He's got two rented horses from the livery stable. He's in the alley beside the hotel, waiting for you."

Again, that odd mixture of relief and disappointment. She almost wished she were riding out to the reservation alone. But this was the wiser avenue.

Rebekah and Jimmy took the back stairs that landed them in

the empty kitchen. They used the back door to quietly make their escape.

Stepping into the deep darkness of the alley disoriented Rebekah momentarily. A hand gripped her elbow, causing her to realize she had tilted and almost stumbled down the back steps.

There was her brother beside her, studying her as she righted herself. By the time her eyes adjusted to the darkness, she could see Jimmy tying Amos's bed roll to his horse. Amos had taken and hooked her medical bag to the saddle horn of one of the horses, her carpetbag dangling off the other side.

Jimmy jerked his thumb over his shoulder to indicate the hotel second floor. "Don't you worry, ma'am, I'll keep him going in circles for the next two days. I don't think we can fool him longer than that, but by then, I'll have met you in Macy and we'll head right on back to McKinnon Ranch. Right, ma'am?"

Doubt tinged Jimmy's voice. She understood it. He wondered if she planned to remain on the reservation for good.

She gave him a strong hug and admonished him to keep up the health regimen she'd outlined for him and squeezed his gangly forearms. "You take good care of yourself, young man."

Jimmy bit his lower lip and Rebekah knew he was far more worried about her than himself. He leaned in and smacked her cheek with a kiss and then pulled back, shoved his hands in his pockets and mumbled, "You take care, Miss Rebekah."

Rebekah tipped forward and kissed him on the cheek before gently patting it.

Turning, she found Amos mounted, staring off into the empty street at the end of the alley. Their family had never been ones to show much affection, even for one another. Rebekah had struggled with wanting that affection, envious of how Susan expressed in letters and in person her deep love and respect for her family, especially her sisters.

In recent months Rebekah, with her dramatic experiences in the west, had felt herself changing inside. She found it simpler to express emotion than she thought it was. That night of holding Jimmy after his knife wound, knowing how close he was to death, had broken and, at the same time, restored her.

Rebekah swung aboard the horse and Jimmy handed off the reins to her. With a small wave, Rebekah followed Amos at a trot out of the alley, down the main street, and out of town. They left Sioux City behind and aimed toward the place of their people—the Omaha Indian Reservation.

CHAPTER 5

Darkness over the prairie was incredible. The only similar experience Rebekah recalled was in the Palo Duro Canyon in West Texas where she and Jimmy had escaped from the Baxter brothers. But on that night, they'd had the bright moon to guide them.

This night, there was no moon, no stars. Thick clouds dipped to the point she couldn't distinguish the horizon from the prairie.

She and Amos would have to feel their way home.

She let Amos take the lead even after they were through the Winnebago Reservation and onto the Omaha Indian Reservation. Though they had both roamed these prairies all their life, Amos had more so than her. Plus, he had spent the last three years there whereas her time on the reservation felt like a distant memory.

Still, the prairie was soft and unchanged and unchanging as it stretched on, the clapping of the horses' hooves hardly disturbing the silence.

Rebekah recognized they were following one of many well-traveled buffalo trails that the deer and the Omaha used to navigate between water sources. This trail, she knew, would lead them south to the front door of Amos' cabin.

For many years, Amos had lived in a teepee, banded together with other young men his age who refused to adopt any semblance of European culture and ways. They were determined to live life as unspoiled and unregulated as they could within the boundaries of the reservation.

It was only in recent years that Amos had settled for building a simple log cabin to use as his home base since he still spent much of his time out on the prairie hunting, fishing, and gathering. He was still living the simple ways Rebekah longed for but knew that she was not meant to live. She was called to a new path for her people, one that made her despised in the eyes of some and a hero to others.

Rebekah settled into a comfortable rhythm with the horse. The vastness of the prairie engulfed her, swallowed her whole and made her feel as though she had disappeared from the world, never to be seen or heard from again.

But it wasn't a frightening feeling. It was just the prairie, with all its wonder. Life went on in all its layers beneath and above her —from the roots that burrowed deep into the ground, to all the organisms tunneling through the good earth, to all that grew on its surface, roamed across it, and flew above it. All working together in harmony as the Creator intended.

The hours wore on. The night grew deeper and even stiller. It stilled her soul, and for the first time in months, she did not feel the need to look over her shoulder. Nothing was hidden from her in the miles of wide-open expanse. No one stalking her. Even the mysterious tail man was far, far behind. So were her reputation and responsibilities and expectations.

There on the prairie, there was so little to do or think about or worry over. It wrapped her in its comfort, leaving her with the feeling of being completely alone yet not isolated.

Time and space lapsed into nothing.

But watching Amos from behind, she realized he seemed to be growing larger. And larger.

Rebekah blinked, then rubbed her sleep deprived eyes. They were gritty, as if the prairie winds had blown dust into them. It had, but she wasn't seeing things.

Amos' outline was growing larger because there was something breaking the horizon ahead of them.

Rebekah shifted in her saddle to see around him. A dark object lay ahead, less than a mile away. Amos's cabin.

She centered in the saddle again, her legs aching from being wrapped around the horse's belly during the long ride.

Amos' form grew impossibly large until they were close enough for the distinctive features of the cabin to materialize in the darkness. Amos pulled up the horse and dismounted with such ease Rebekah's whole body ached. Amos didn't offer to help her down, though he certainly would have if Rebekah asked.

She wouldn't dream of asking. Even as a little girl, she had wanted her brother to think she was as strong and nimble and quick as he.

That was not easy to prove tonight, but Rebekah dismounted with only a short pause as she gripped the saddle horn until her legs grew firm beneath her. She retrieved her medical bag while Amos unhooked her carpetbag from the other side. Their eyes met over the saddle, then he led the way inside the cabin.

Rebekah followed then stood still so as not to trip on anything on the dirt floor. She had not been in Amos' cabin in many years.

He lit a candle and placed it atop his wood-burning stove. He gestured to the stove, then headed back outside to tend the horses.

Rebekah went to the stove, rubbing her hands together. She hadn't realized how cold they'd grown on the ride through the prairie.

Rebekah warmed her hands with the candle's flame, stretching her fingers from her claw grip on the reins. Flexing her fingers a final time, she set about starting a fire in the stove as Amos had indicated. They could communicate so much without words, yet so little with words.

Rebekah had the fire coaxed to life by the time Amos entered the cabin, securing the door against the remaining night. It would be dawn soon and they would continue on to Susan's place where she lived and cared for her mother at Logan Creek.

Stomach rumbling, Rebekah recalled how Amos hadn't eaten a hot meal at the hotel. This was an opportunity to see he ate something to nourish him.

She poked around the cabinet near the stove and found a jar of chicken stock. She warmed it in the only pan he owned, adding a few dried herbs from her medical bag.

There was no bed in the cabin but Amos produced a buffalo hide from one corner and made a pallet near the stove. Then he settled on the only chair in the room, a three-legged stool he'd fashioned himself. A basket sat beside it and he retrieved material from it. It appeared to be a beading project, but Rebekah couldn't tell what he was making.

She ladled two bowls of the broth and set one on the floor beside his basket before settling on the buffalo hide pallet, legs tucked under her in as lady like fashion as she could manage. It felt out of place in this setting, as much as her city made dress did. As much as she did.

She was home at last on the Omaha Indian Reservation. Her dream. And yet she felt lost.

She ate her broth, then stretched her arms and her neck before wrapping up in the buffalo hide.

She listened to the quiet click of wood spoon against the pottery bowl as Amos ate. It sounded like he dipped up a second helping, but she wasn't sure.

Reality and her dreams blended into a vision of the prairie with a red moon on the horizon, shining on a lone buffalo standing against the wind.

CHAPTER 6

Warm fingers caressing her eyelids awoke Rebekah. Her lips turned up in a smile at the gentleness, the comforting feel. Then her mind caught up and her eyes snapped open to discover who was touching her. She found it was a beam of sunlight.

Her movements slow, Rebekah pushed herself upright on the buffalo hide. She blinked against the sunbeam to find the cabin empty. Amos must have gone outside to prepare the horses for their continued journey across the prairie to reach Susan at Logan Creek.

Rebekah didn't relish the thought of getting back in the saddle, but remembering the urgency of her mission propelled her to her feet, albeit slowly. She stretched, gingerly, and tried to smooth her rumpled clothing. Useless. Kneeling on the floor again, she retrieved a fresh suit of clothes from her carpetbag. She quickly changed and went to the stove to stoke the fire and start breakfast.

Right when she finished washing the bowls from last night, Amos came through the door, his beading project in hand. She had wondered why he was taking so long with the horses, then

34

realized he must have found a place outside to work on his project. The aroma of the meal brought him in.

She still couldn't tell what it was and didn't want to ask, but she knew where he had been.

Cow Creek a quarter mile from the cabin, a creek that served as the flowing boundary line between her allotted land and his. They had both received 160 acres courtesy of the Omaha Allotment Act.

For now, Rebekah had leased her farmland to an Omaha neighbor to plant a corn crop each year. Her portion of the harvest went toward books and supplies for the children at the Omaha Agency boarding school in Macy.

Rebekah dished up two bowls of grits and started to offer Amos one. She noticed his shoulders shake with a suppressed cough and she placed the bowls back on the stove and retrieved her medical bag instead.

Before she could open it, though, Amos held up a hand and she lowered it back to the floor. He had never allowed her to treat him for his tuberculosis despite her many attempts to do so. They had been distant for many years and now, he refused to even let her touch him. To care for him.

She never had a more difficult patient than her brother.

Rebekah handed him his bowl from the stove and remained standing to eat hers. So did he. There was a feeling of movement between them. Her time on the reservation was short.

The silence was uncomfortable. There was so much to say between them that neither of them had anything to say.

Nearly finished eating, Rebekah broke the silence with a question they both already knew the answer to. "It will take us about three hours to ride to Susan's, won't it?"

"No."

Rebekah arched an eyebrow at her brother. He finished eating before elaborating.

"Susan no longer lives with her mother. She is in Bancroft with her husband."

If she wasn't so accustomed to maintaining her composure, Rebekah's knees would have buckled. "Her *husband?* In *Bancroft?*"

She didn't know which shocked her more—that her dear friend was married, or that she lived in a town off the reservation.

Rebekah couldn't finish her grits as she tried to process this news. Yes, she had been away from the reservation for three years, but how was it possible she didn't know Susan had married? Her friend who, as two Omaha Indian women, had gone through medical school with hardly one conversation about marriage. It wasn't something either of them thought was realistic.

Susan once wrote home, "So I will be a dear little old maid we read of in books…I shall…come and see you all and doctor and dose you all. Won't that be fine?"

The news of Susan marrying was both devastating and exhilarating for Rebekah. But she couldn't sort out either of those feelings. Not yet.

"Well," she said, dipping her bowl into a pan of clean water, "We best be on our way. Bancroft is just as far as Logan Creek from here."

Within minutes, Rebekah and Amos were in the saddle and on their way south on the sunflower spotted prairie. The clouds played hide-and-seek with the sun, covering it some of the time, letting it peek through others, and then completely abandoning it. Geese dove for the floor of the prairie, backsides in the air as they swooped in search of the perfect landing spot. Apparently not finding it, they banked and were sky bound once again. Rebekah watched another flock make a dive, their silhouettes tracing the rolling mound-like terrain of the Nebraskan prairie.

An hour into the ride, Rebekah noted a different sort of movement to her left. Two human figures were barely distinct with the green hillside behind them. They walked at a purposeful pace on an intersect course with Rebekah and Amos, though at least a half mile away. Amos, whose head turned enough to assure Rebekah he had seen them, kept their steady, single file pace.

Time passed slow as the figures' steps matched the clop, clop of the horses hooves across the alive prairie. She nudged her horse up to a trot to reach Amos' side, where she slowed and nodded toward the figures.

"Who are they?"

They were close enough now for Rebekah to see they were two young men. They were dressed in farm clothes with wide felt brim hats shielding them from the sun. Whoever they were, they lived close enough to reach this section by foot, a section Amos was most familiar with.

Gaze still trained on their destination, Amos said, "The Fremont brothers."

Rebekah waited, hoping he would offer a guess as to why these young men kept their path angled in a way to intercept Rebekah and her brother.

Amos said nothing more, so Rebekah lapsed into her own imaginings of why these two young men wanted to catch up with her brother.

When they finally reached the intersecting point, Amos pulled his horse to a halt and dismounted. It would be rude to talk down to his fellow tribesmen.

Rebekah dismounted as well, staying between the horses as she gingerly stretched. She wouldn't mind if their conversation lasted a while. This might be the only break she and Amos took on the long ride to Susan's.

The young men halted and exchanged greetings with Amos in the Umoho language. To her surprise, she heard her name come from one of the Fremonts.

Ducking, she peered beneath the horse's neck to find the brothers staring at her. Still holding the reins of her horse, she led him around in front of Amos' and greeted the young men. This close, she recognized the former gangly and sometimes troublesome boys who lived further north on Cow Creek. Twins, they were the oldest of the family of 12 which included a grandfather and their father. Their mother had died in childbirth shortly before Rebekah left the reservation. She had been too late to help during her difficult delivery.

The boys had the same grim expression on their faces now as they did when Rebekah arrived at their cabin after their mother's death.

The one she knew as Alvin addressed her. "Our father needs you, Doc Beck."

Oh, how long it had been since she was called that by one of her own people! She cleared emotion from her throat. "What's happened?"

Alvin hesitated, trying to find the right words. He pointed to the sky, squinting against the sun, then swept his arm across the prairie. "Father was plowing yesterday and fell to the ground. The sun was very hot. We knew your brother brought you from Wyoming. We came out to find you."

Rebekah frowned. She could offer a fair guess on Mr. Fremont's illness, but she couldn't be sure without seeing him herself.

But the Fremont farm was in the opposite direction of Susan.

Susan, the one who had drawn Rebekah back to the reservation, caused her to risk everything to try and save her life.

And now, here was another life in danger. If Mr. Fremont did suffer from a heat stroke, Rebekah needed to tend him right away.

Rebekah nodded at the boys. "Lead the way."

To speed up the journey, Rebekah suggested the Fremont boys ride double on Rebekah's horse. She intended to double up with Amos.

Her brother wouldn't allow it and simply let her ride while he led the horse. He was determined they wouldn't get close on this trip. Maybe never again.

It took two hours to reach the Fremont cabin. The small barn, kitchen garden, and henhouse were the extent of the family's wealth aside from the vast farmland they worked together. It was unchanged from her last visit when she had arrived in time to pronounce the mother of the house and her baby dead. Rebekah hoped that wasn't the reason she was here this time, to do nothing more than offer a few words of comfort to the family again.

Inside the cabin, they were welcomed by the scent of pork chops frying and the solemn face of the boys' grandfather. It wasn't meal time, which told her the grandfather had seen them coming and wanted to offer all they could for her services. Rebekah greeted him with a nod and indicated the blanket that covered the door to one of the other rooms in the cabin. The old man nodded and Rebekah entered it, medical bag in hand to do what she could to prevent more grief in this house.

Three hours later, Rebekah emerged with a heavy sigh. The family was gathered around the table, pork chops dried out on the stove. Rebekah rolled down her sleeves, meeting the eyes of each family member in turn.

"With proper care and bed rest, he should make a full recovery within a few weeks."

The relief in the room wasn't visible, but the power of it swept over her.

The grandfather rose and went to a worn wooden chest in one corner of the room. He opened it and withdrew a deer hide bundle. Laying it on the floor, he flipped back the corners to reveal what was likely a lifetime of treasure: an antler bone-handled knife polished to a shine; a hawk feather fan with a beaded handle; a turtle carved from stone; and a coin that dated back to the first half of the century and fur trapper days.

Rebekah knelt on the floor across from the grandfather as she observed each precious piece. She reached out and touched the turtle, feeling the comforting coolness of its stone back. She had lived most of her life at breakneck speed, something that was neither healthy for her nor the people she served. The turtle reminded her of Susan — the steady worker who never faltered, never hurried, and somehow managed to accomplish so much within each of her days.

Rebekah rested the turtle in the palm of her hand. She observed it, the fine way the details of its face had been etched in the stone. Holding it up between her and the grandfather, she met his eyes and he nodded. He approved of her choice of payment.

Rebekah shifted to rise, only to find her knees buckling. Strong hands on her shoulders from behind steadied and lifted her from the floor. Before she could turn her head, Amos had already retreated several steps back.

The day mostly spent, Rebekah was anxious to get back in the saddle and continue their journey to Susan. But the sound of hoofbeats coming at a gallop set her heart to fluttering. Surely the tail man hadn't already found her?

Amos must have had the same thought, because he pressed himself against the wall of the cabin to peer carefully behind the thin curtain covering the front window. He looked at her and shook his head. It wasn't the danger Rebekah feared.

Alvin opened the door to the visitor. It was one of her people, someone she vaguely recognized. He looked directly at her.

"Doc Beck. My niece needs you."

Rebekah closed her eyes, exhaling. Between the vastness of the prairie and her peoples' needs, she might never make it to Susan. At least, not before the mystery man caught up to her.

CHAPTER 7

"I'll have the sirloin steak—biggest one you've got—medium rare, three rolls with honey..."

Jimmy ran his eyes up and down the menu as the waitress stood rooted next to his corner table. He couldn't read the name of this fancy restaurant in Sioux City, but Miss Rebekah had taught him to read well enough to make out the vast array of options on the menu he clutched. It had him near dizzy.

Besides, he was plumb worn out. He'd spent the day leading the tail man on wild goose chases, all the while convincing the man that Rebekah and Amos were still in Sioux City. His head felt unnaturally light, but nothing a good meal wouldn't fix.

Miss Rebekah had told him he was very blessed that the knife missed all his vital organs. The one Jimmy was most grateful for was the fact that the knife had missed his stomach.

Back on the ranch, Stubby liked to say that Jimmy would eat anything that, "don't eat him first." That wasn't entirely true. Jimmy preferred his food cooked when possible.

He hummed. "These little garlic potatoes sure sound good. And you say these green beans are fancy? I'll take some of those, too, and the cooked carrots. Oh, and a side of ham with these mashed yams, and add on a roll of that highfalutin sausage you say comes from...one of them countries that ain't France." Jimmy looked up from the menu at the old waitress who just stared at him as if she had never seen a creature like him before. Maybe she hadn't.

"Anything else?"

Jimmy looked at the menu, wondering what he could have missed. "I reckon not, ma'am. Just make it two of all that."

He heard a thump on the table and looked up to see the waitress scrambling to pick up the tablet she'd dropped. She whipped the menu out of his hand and stomped away. Jimmy tugged on the bottom corners of his fringed buckskin jacket—a gift from the famous gunfighter Cord Johnson—to straighten it. He licked his palms and smoothed his hair back.

The waitress probably thought he didn't have the money to pay for all the food he ordered. He should set her mind at ease about it. Laramie had loaded Jimmy with a fist full of paper money in a coin bag. Laramie had wanted to make sure Jimmy was well supplied to look after Miss Rebekah on this trip. If anything, getting rid of some of the money made him feel better. Less to lose if he got bushwhacked.

Sioux City wasn't a particularly dangerous town. What made Jimmy's skin crawl was the man seated at the opposite side of the restaurant, facing him but never looking his way. The tail man hadn't stayed on Jimmy all day, opting to spend a good bit of his time in the hotel lobby, waiting for Miss Rebekah to come down the stairs. Jimmy snorted to himself. The man would have a longer wait then he had the patience for.

Speaking of which, Jimmy needed to come up with new ruses for tomorrow to keep the man occupied. He was going to lose patience eventually with the phantom doctor and do something that uncovered the truth.

Jimmy folded his hands in front of him on the table, spinning his thumbs together as he stared at them. The action gave him something to do other than think about what he was doing. It didn't help, and Jimmy once again went over everything that had happened since last night.

While he'd been careful not to tell any lies, a practice he couldn't stomach, he *was* deceiving this man by leading him on wild goose chases and tricking him into thinking Miss Rebekah was still in town.

But then, wasn't there a story in the Bible about a woman who hid the Hebrew spies or something?

A sudden thunk jarred him. The waitress had returned and plopped down the first plate of his order. Jimmy sat back, his turn to stare with mouth agape as she slid another plate from her elbow onto the table, and then two more from her other arm. She had somehow carried four plates all by herself. How about that!

And then she stepped to the side.

Another waitress was behind her and plunked down four more plates.

Jimmy stared at the feast filling up the whole table in front of him.

The waitress snapped, "Anything *else*?"

Jimmy looked around at all the plates. Everything seemed just as he'd ordered, so he answered, "Just some ketchup, please, ma'am. And what do you have for dessert?"

CHAPTER 8

It was the following morning before Rebekah and Amos departed the third little log house since they had left his. News of her arrival was spreading like a prairie fire across the reservation, something that terrified her. Uncle Robert knew this would happen, knew it would become a well-known fact that Doctor Rebekah LaRoche had returned to the Omaha Indian Reservation after Roger Graham banned her for life.

Yet, despite the fear, Rebekah felt no regrets. In this third cabin, she had treated an elderly Omaha woman who was dying. Conventional medicine would do nothing for her, so Rebekah opted for soothing remedies passed down to her through her grandmother. That, and prayers. The woman was a Christian and faithful attender of the local church until she grew too ill to make the ten-mile trek.

Her face was one of joy when Rebekah retrieved her New Testament out of her medical bag and read to her from the Gospel of John. No one in the elder's family could read and the woman told Rebekah, tears in her eyes, that she had been without the Word for so long.

It was another of the tremendous services Susan brought to

their people. Beyond her gifting as a healer, Susan took care of her people's spiritual needs along with their physical ones. Susan was known to hang a lantern in her window to guide people to her. There was always someone who needed her.

They needed Rebekah, too.

That was why she had left her home all those years ago to attend school and then medical college. All to bring it back to serve her people.

It had been a heady experience for her as a young Omaha girl going out into white civilization to learn their ways, and help her people adapt to the new world they lived in. Not everything she learned benefited her people, but much of it did.

All of that had been stripped from them one fateful night.

And there she was again, come full circle back to her people. How soon would Graham hear of her return and come to throw her off the reservation himself? Was the tail man someone he had sent to do the deed? That wasn't the only possibility, but Rebekah felt in her spirit it was true. Her time among her people was running out. How fast depended on how long Jimmy could keep the man occupied. He was a talented young man, but even he had his limits.

The urgency overpowering her, Rebekah nudged her horse into a lope. Amos matched her pace and they found a rhythm to cover the earth and the distance between herself and Susan. They left the boundaries of the reservation. Not far now.

Alternating speeds to give their horses rest, Rebekah could hardly believe her eyes when they finally crested a hill and Bancroft lay in view before them. She breathed a sigh of relief. No one else had intercepted them and she was at last nearing her dear friend's home.

Cold fear tangled in Rebekah's heated chest. What if Susan had already slipped away?

Taking to a lope again, Rebekah and Amos soon reached

Bancroft, where Rebekah slowed her horse to allow him to take the lead to Susan's house. It wasn't far.

Rebekah found Susan lived in a wood-framed house in Bancroft, across from the small Presbyterian church. A fruit orchard and garden took up most of the modest yard. A sign hung near the front door, announcing Susan's private practice from within her home.

Rebekah doubted Susan had had much opportunity to practice at home. Like Rebekah yesterday, Susan must still spend most of her time traveling the prairie in blazing heat and blinding snow storms to care for her people. Until she fell so desperately ill.

Rebekah hastily dismounted in front of the house, willing her legs to hold her steady as she unstrapped her medical bag and made for the front door. Amos followed.

Forcing herself up the steps, Rebekah raised a hand to knock on the door only to have it swing inward before she reached it.

There stood Rosalie, unmoving as she stared at Rebekah. Then she flung her arms wide and Rebekah fell into them, gripping tight to her friend and accomplished woman in her own right.

Rebekah whispered near Rosalie's ear, "Am I in time?"

Rosalie pulled back and pressed her warm palms on Rebekah's cheeks. She nodded resolutely. "Susan is strong. But I am so glad you are here."

They went up the stairs where a door stood open to the right of the hall. Rosalie stood to one side of the door and swept her hand in a gentle arc to allow Rebekah to enter first. She did, her sole focus on the woman in the bed whose dove eyes and soft expression filled the room with love. Hope.

Rebekah rushed across the short space between them and engulfed Susan, pressing her cheek against her friend's, willing her own health into this beloved woman.

Rebekah pulled back and pressed her palms on each side of Susan's cheeks, then on her neck, her forehead, her chin, her ears.

Rebekah's tears dripped onto Susan's morning gown as she used her fingers to brush wisps of hair away from Susan's face before caressing her cheeks again. Susan touched Rebekah's hands, so little strength in her arms that Rebekah's heart fell. But there was still Susan's smile, assuring her that no matter what happened, all would be well. Someday.

Rebekah's lips parted, but no words came out. Not even a simple greeting. As always, Susan was there to fill the gap of her deficiencies.

"Rebekah. You have come." Susan's hands slipped and Rebekah grasped them tenderly and situated them across Susan's midsection. "You would do no less for me."

Susan inhaled, trembling. "There is so much I must tell you. There is so much I have left undone. I have a hygiene regimen that I am teaching throughout the reservation. I've already incorporated it into the school at Macy and through churches, but the outlying corners of the reservation are in need of regular check-ins. Also, there is a file cabinet in my office with legal document references and lease agreements, and for those who need to apply for treatment I cannot give them here. Dear Rebekah, the stench of alcohol and all its destruction has our people in its clutches. We must banish it, we must! Oh, and at the church, the Bible study, I was teaching through Acts, of the suffering of the apostles and the early church..."

Susan's voice gave out. Rosalie retrieved a glass of water next to Susan's bed and Rebekah cradled Susan's head while she drank. After a few moments of silence, Susan's gaze faltered. She used one hand to cover Rebekah's that remained on hers. She rubbed Rebekah's hand as though she were the one who needed comfort and care.

"Rebekah. You are truly one of God's lovely women. I know He will restore you to our people someday. You are beloved here."

Rebekah set her jaw, determined not to weep. Not on her

friend who had stayed true to their calling, who had served their people with so much dedication it nearly killed her.

Rebekah gripped Susan's hands hard then released them. "You will continue to care for our people. You are of too great of value for God to allow anything else."

Rebekah wanted to believe this with all of her heart.

Susan tried to smile. "The mothers back in Connecticut are concerned about my decision earlier this year. To marry. But dear Rebekah! I have no regrets."

Susan opened her palm and placed it across her stomach, tightening her morning dress. Rebekah's heart leapt. "You...you are with child." A statement by an experienced physician, not a stunned friend.

She spent two hours giving Susan a meticulous exam and prescribing a list of remedies for them to implement right away. Susan suffered from a chronic ear disease that was a miserable mystery affecting so many parts of her and rendering her bedridden and nearly deaf. And very much pregnant.

Susan was indeed of the Upstream People—the ones who went against the current.

Susan's eyelids fluttered, and Rebekah stroked her fingers over them, giving Susan permission to close them and rest.

Rebekah stepped out of the room, Rosalie coming as well and closing Susan's door quietly behind them. Rebekah turned to her and her knees failed. Rosalie caught her under the arms and helped lower her to the floor with Amos' help. Rebekah leaned into the wall, palms pressed to her eyes as she wept silently.

She didn't know how long it took for the initial wave of grief and desperation to pass, but it finally did. Rosalie was there, kneeling on the floor and offering a handkerchief and a strong hand on her shoulder.

"Rebekah. Please stay and treat the patients who come in every day desperate for Susan's help. If you can only remain one week, it would make a tremendous difference. Not only for them, but in setting Susan's mind at ease, knowing you are fulfilling her role for this time."

One week. Even one day could jeopardize Rebekah's ultimate return to the reservation if the tail man caught up with her. Or worse. Roger Graham himself.

Rosalie understood and touched Rebekah's cheek with one finger, tender as she would her own sister's. "I know there is so much risk for you even being here. You could lose everything if you are caught."

"We will not be caught."

The sudden sound of her brother's gravelly voice caused Rebekah to inhale sharply. All his words stunned her. But one word struck her in the heart.

We.

CHAPTER 9

Something wasn't right. Something that *already* wasn't right, wasn't right. Jimmy could feel it in his bones as he watched the tail man heading for the hotel.

Just the way the man gave a quick look to each side told Jimmy something wasn't right as he hid behind a blue silk dress on a mannequin displayed in the front window of the General Store. The tail man was looking to make sure Jimmy wasn't around. Which was why Jimmy was hiding behind a woman's skirt for the first time in his life.

Satisfied, the man strode into the hotel as Jimmy watched from across the street.

Time to move. Jimmy started to leave his cover when he heard loud throat clearing behind him. He whipped around because the throat clearing sounded awfully feminine.

It was.

The young shopkeeper's daughter glared at him. Jimmy had managed to avoid her checking him out with his purchases over the past two days. He always stalled at one shelf or another until her father was free and could tally Jimmy's items. But she had him now, arms crossed as she stared down her pointed nose at him.

"You have a girl you're buying that for?"

Mortified, Jimmy realized she was talking about the dress. In focusing on the tail man across the street, he had absently run his hand down the skirt and now held it by the hem. Jimmy released it like it was fire, and tried to stutter an explanation, but nothing sensible came out. He lifted his hat off at the girl and dashed out the door.

Running across the street, Jimmy didn't heed the fact that the tail man might be sitting by one of the hotel lobby windows, watching for him. After wild goose chases all over town—Jimmy taking plates of food to the hotel, sending telegrams to Doctor McKinnon indicating that Rebekah was still in town, buying medical supplies for her trip to the reservation—the tail man was getting suspicious. He might be watching for Jimmy now, but Jimmy's gut told him otherwise. And his gut told him to hurry.

He burst into the lobby, drawing the attention of a plump woman who was standing in line at the hotel desk, fresh off the train. Jimmy didn't know what to do about her askance look other than lift his hat off his head again and dart by her and for the stairs.

The tail man wasn't in the lobby.

Jimmy took the stairs two at a time and came to an abrupt halt at the top. He tiptoed down the hall to reach the corner leading to Miss Rebekah's room where she was still checked in as a guest.

Jimmy whipped his hat off and peeked around the corner with one eye. The tail man was at Miss Rebekah's door, ear pressed against it, face turned away from Jimmy. The man pulled back and so did Jimmy, knowing he would take another look over his shoulder. Counting to three, Jimmy peeked around the corner again. The tail man rapped softly on Miss Rebekah's door. He waited, listening, and then dropped to one knee, inserting something into the lock. The man was a professional, all right, and had the door open in seconds. He was inside in a blink.

Jimmy gulped. He had to act fast. It wouldn't take the tail man long to see that Rebekah's things were missing.

"What do you think you are doing, young man?"

Jimmy whirled to find the plump woman glaring at him, carpetbag in one hand and closed parasol in the other. The parasol rested on her shoulder, ready for her to take a hard swing at his head.

This woman was exactly who Jimmy needed.

He jerked his thumb over his shoulder to indicate the hallway around the corner. "Ma'am, there's a man who has been harassing my friend. She's in room 203 and I think he just went in there."

The plump woman's eyes widened as she took in a sharp breath. Yep. This was exactly what Jimmy needed.

"I'll run for the sheriff if you'll keep an eye on the door here?"

"Oh, Sonny, I'll do more than that. You just stand back."

The woman stormed around the corner and Jimmy ran for the stairs. He leapt down them three at a time, landing with a hard thunk that rattled him to the top of his head. His lungs were burning and so was a particular spot in his gut. But he ignored it all as he ran for the door, flinging it open and hollering, "Sheriff! Where's the sheriff?"

Jimmy ran up the street toward the jail, only to hear someone hollering from behind him, calling out that the sheriff was coming.

Jimmy skidded to a halt and ran back toward the hotel, seeing the sheriff striding in that direction. Jimmy tried to leap the three steps of the hotel entrance, but failed, the tip of his boot catching the top step and sending him sprawling across the porch.

Helpful hands grabbed his arms and hauled him to his feet, heightening the pain in his gut and his head.

The hotel's double doors swirled in his vision, moving away from him as he tried to point at them. "Sheriff, a man just broke into a woman's room. I saw him pick the lock."

Jimmy didn't know whether he was pointing at the hotel door, the boardwalk, or the sky, but the sheriff must have gotten the message. He was gone and Jimmy staggered toward the door, helpful hands from two men guiding him inside. He blinked, his vision and ringing ears clearing enough for him to make out the scene on the staircase.

The tail man was stumbling down the steps, arms over his head to try and shield it from the plump woman who whacked him mercilessly with her parasol.

"You cad! You peeping Tom, you! Why, if I caught you breaking into my room like that, you wouldn't have eyeballs left to see with or a head to put them in!"

Jimmy, still supported on each side, gulped down his relief as the sheriff rescued the tail man by clamping a handcuff on each wrist, pinning the man's hands behind his back. He nodded at the woman. "I'll take it from here, ma'am. This fellow won't be bothering any more ladies at this hotel."

Jimmy tried to stand up straight when the sheriff passed with the tail man in tow. The man glared at him, the first time they had made eye contact in their two-day cat and mouse game. Jimmy couldn't fathom it, but a silly grin spread over his face as he managed to lift his hat off his head and salute the man.

He dropped it back in place and rubbed his forehead with a groan. The plump woman stood in front of him, ruined parasol resting on one shoulder. "You're ill, young man. Best get on over to the doctor."

"Aw, thank you ma'am, but I'm just fine. Got more work to do..." Jimmy shook his head.

Bad idea. The room swirled and pitched. Those helpful hands were the only way he stayed on his feet as the room blinked out to black.

CHAPTER 10

Sunlight filtered through the stained-glassed windows of the Presbyterian church in Walthill on the reservation. The light cast an array of color across the shiny wood pews. The blues, reds, yellows, and greens reminded Rebekah of the prairie in springtime, that explosion of wildflowers dancing in the wind to unheard sounds of heaven's symphony.

That was how Rebekah thought of the prairie when she was a little girl. She held tight to that image now as she pressed her fist into the small of her back and stretched long and deep. She heard a wagon rolling up even as hoofbeats pounded away from the church. A man had ridden in that morning with his sick little boy in the saddle in front of him, and Rebekah had just finished treating him. Now there was the sound of more patients coming in.

The past two days had been incredible. Amos had used his lifetime of connections throughout the reservation to install what Rebekah could only describe as a mobile, underground medical network. They had four designated locations on the reservation for her to practice out of, and Amos and his longtime friends secretly spread the word to their people that Rebekah was there to take care of their needs.

One of the locations was this Presbyterian church. Today, it served as Rebekah's medical clinic where she would treat patients until three in the afternoon. Then she would move to a store room behind a trading post thirty miles away.

Amos had enlisted the help of his friends to cart patients in, drop them off for treatment, and move the horses and wagons away. Should the tail man or Graham show up unexpectedly, he would not see a cluster of vehicles in a place where they shouldn't be.

Not that there was much risk of anyone arriving unannounced. Amos had designated a horde of young men, including the Fremonts, to watch the main roads leading into the reservation and the roads leading to their designated locations.

If only they could make it last for a whole week. Better yet, a lifetime for Rebekah.

The door opened and in came a young couple, shy as they approached Rebekah. She didn't know them personally and understood why they might feel intimidated. She was one of few who had ever set foot off the reservation for education back east. Not only that, she had spent the last three years traveling the West on medical missions in places they had only heard stories about. Deserts, mountains, ranches tens of thousands of acres in size.

Rebekah smiled as warmly as her tired lips would allow. She spread her hands in a welcoming gesture. "Please, have a seat and tell me how I might help you."

They sat together, though not too close. The young man, wearing a starched white shirt, tie, and what must have been his best pair of trousers, clenching his felt hat in hand. He stared at the back of the pew, mouth hanging open and lips moving but no words came out.

Neither of them appeared ill, but Rebekah was tempted to

check the young man for a fever. He was sweating profusely despite the coolness of the day and the comfortable temperature inside the church.

Rebekah seated herself on the pew in front of them, arms resting on the back of it as she waited.

The young man swallowed and a sound came from his throat, a high grunt, no words. He tried again but the young woman burst out, "We want to get married legally."

Rebekah pressed her lips together to seal off her amused smile. The two could get married there at the church, but a legal marriage license required paperwork and filing with the Indian agent. Susan kept all the documentation they needed on hand.

But Susan did more than paperwork for young couples. She served in the role of pre-marital counseling to make sure young Indian couples were prepared for the responsibility they were taking on with marriage and starting a family.

Rebekah couldn't help much in that department, though. She lacked Susan's wisdom.

All she could ask was, "Have you prayed over your decision?"

The young man crushed his hat harder and the young woman stared at Rebekah, jaw slack. Rebekah reached out and patted her hand.

"That is what I advise you to do and this is the place for it. Please, use the front pew and don't mind anyone else who comes in. Take your time. Tomorrow I will be back near Doc Sue's place and will prepare the document you need if you decide to make this lifelong commitment."

Three p.m. and four patients later, the young couple was still in the front pew when Rebekah left the church. She didn't know if she would see them tomorrow, but she hoped in her spirit they would find the right way.

Amos waited for her outside, horses saddled and ready. She mounted and they set out at a trot for the trading post.

They were halfway there when Amos pulled his horse to a

sudden halt. Rebekah did as well, heart quickening. She looked around and behind them at the empty prairie. They were nearing a crest that Rebekah couldn't see over. Had Amos heard or sensed something on the other side?

She looked at him, questioningly. He nodded at the crest. "Do you wish to stop there?"

Rebekah didn't understand. They were still miles from the trading post where patients would already be waiting for her. It didn't make sense to stop and camp now in the middle of the day.

Amos stared at the crest and Rebekah did too. The wind gusted, flattening the grasses at the top to reveal three large boulders set against the blue sky.

Rebekah inhaled, moisture stinging her eyes from the wind, and memories. She recognized where they were and knew why Amos hadn't explained.

She nudged her horse ahead of his, taking the crest at a soft lope. She pulled her horse up next to the boulders and halted. Dismounting onto the tallest one, its flat edge slanting toward the earth, she found her balance and stood up straight and tall here at one of the highest points on the land her father had farmed until his death. She closed her eyes and turned her face toward the sun, inhaled, and released it all. She knelt on the rock and she peered over the side.

A pile of rocks lay in a rectangle, determined prairie grasses growing between them. The grave was snugged close and safe to the three boulders that would always mark its location.

Rebekah pressed her hands on her knees and bowed her head. "I've returned, Father."

CHAPTER 11

There were no long customer lines inside the St. Louis Union Station this time. Roger Graham strode straight to one of the windows. He didn't offer a smile or chitchat with the young man stamping his ticket.

This wasn't a time for charm.

There were only two things on Graham's mind: the telegram in one coat pocket that came from Sioux City. His hired man had landed himself in jail for breaking into a woman's room. At least that was how the newspapers reported it. All his man said was that he had been falsely accused and was in jail. That left Rebekah LaRoche free to travel unmonitored onto the Omaha Indian Reservation.

The second item on Graham's mind was a letter in response to his from the governor of Nebraska. The governor was hesitant to weigh in on the matter, but he assured Graham that if he found Dr. LaRoche on the reservation, the governor would send military to have her removed.

Graham crammed the ticket into his pocket next to the letter. His mother was still on her deathbed with perhaps only hours to live. Graham could not help that. His being there with his mother would not save her, but his destroying Rebekah LaRoche would save lives in the future.

If he had expelled her from the reservation before that fateful night, his wife and daughter would still be alive.

CHAPTER 12

The layers of the broad sky took Rebekah's breath away as she departed the trading post storeroom at sunset. The view was extraordinary.

A full moon hung low in the sky like in her dream, rising from the horizon as the sunset cast glows of warm orange and pink. Layered above, the indigo sky deepened to a black charcoal sprinkled with tiny white dots of a million stars.

A horse stomped its hoof, and she went to where it waited, mounting up next to Amos. Wordlessly, they trotted away from the storeroom, breaking the serenity of that moment of beauty. Rebekah tried to recapture it in her heart, but her mind was filled with the exhaustion and frustrations of the day.

At the storeroom, she had treated patients and helped fill out paperwork the trading post had been holding for an elder who needed to buy a plow for his farm. The red tape of filling out paperwork to access his own money to buy a plow so he could work his own farm was an undue burden on the old man who could neither read nor write. He had been patiently waiting for Doctor Sue to help him since he did not trust anyone who did not speak his language.

Rebekah was appalled to learn his plow had broken down in the spring and he'd been trying to get a new one since then. She wondered if all the paperwork would be processed in time for spring planting next year.

Rebekah had also treated injuries caused by a fight between two men the night before. She knew immediately that they had been drinking. Alcohol was something her father was vehemently opposed to, the same as Susan's father and Susan herself. Susan was on a mighty mission to have it eradicated from the reservation, but it was a difficult battle. One thing Susan would never do, though, was quit. She would die first.

Tomorrow morning, Rebekah would pay her friend another visit. Susan had made Rebekah promise not to hover over her but instead care for all the patients piling up around the reservation. That would do more for Susan—body and soul—than Rebekah staying in her room around the clock, though she wanted to with all her being.

Shifting her mind away from the gloom, Rebekah recalled the story of when she and Susan were in medical school and the students—male and female—watched their first autopsy. One of the young men had fainted. Susan thought it was silly for men to think women couldn't be doctors. The memory made Rebekah chuckle now.

"I would like to laugh."

Rebekah glanced over at Amos who kept looking straight ahead. "I was just thinking of Susan and our time back east with the men at the university. Nothing fazes her. What a mighty warrior she has become for our people."

The last part Rebekah said quietly, knowing Amos did not agree. He had respect for Susan and the things she had done for their people. But he never approved of how the young women had brought so much of the white world into theirs.

Rebekah didn't suppose her brother would ever accept that the white world was there to stay.

They rode in silence the remainder of the evening, arriving well past suppertime at a teepee set up on a low plain. This was the halfway point between them and their next destination. Rebekah was so tired, she couldn't remember where that was.

There was a fire going outside the teepee, tended by Charlie. The middle-aged Omaha man had been one of the ones who brought agent Graham's wife and daughter in after the tragic buggy accident. Rebekah was relieved to see him and hurried to dismount. Charlie was supposed to fetch Jimmy from Macy where her young friend was supposed to meet her yesterday.

What worried her was the fact that Jimmy was nowhere to be seen. Maybe he was inside the teepee?

"Jimmy?" she called out.

Charlie stood and shook his head. "I did not find your white friend in Macy."

Rebekah's heart plummeted. What would have prevented him from making it to Macy? A dozen possibilities swarmed in her head, none of them good.

"Are you certain he wasn't there, Charlie? He was wearing a fringed buskin jacket, cowboy boots..."

She halted at Charlie's darkened look. He wasn't someone who needed his work double checked. If Jimmy were in Macy, Charlie would have found him and convinced him to come with the brief note Rebekah had sent along.

"We will look again tomorrow." Amos said the words with such finality all Rebekah could do was set herself down on the ground by the fire and wait while Charlie ladled up their supper.

❧❦❧

DEEP INTO THE NIGHT, sleepless, Rebekah slipped her shawl around her shoulders and cast aside the hide flap of the teepee. She found Amos still up and sitting by the fire. He was beading again. Charlie snored softly from the other side of the fire.

Rebekah settled near Amos, stretching her hands out to enjoy the fire's warmth on the cool prairie night.

Tension thickened the air between the siblings, broken only by Amos' suppressed cough.

Enough.

"It was not your fault," Rebekah said.

Amos looked up sharply with as close to surprise on his expression as she'd ever seen. She added firmly, "You did a good thing that night. It was not the alcohol in your blood nor the disease that causes your cough that killed Agent Graham's little girl. There are studies going on even now that humans have different blood types and the wrong one is what causes blood transfusions to fail."

Amos looked down again, yanking hard on his string and nearly snapping it. She might as well be speaking in Spanish instead of medical jargon.

"What I mean is, it was not my fault, and it was not your fault. I know this for certain."

"I do not drink now."

That was good to learn. Thinking back, Rebekah recalled how her brother was more clear-eyed the day she left than she had seen him since he was a teenager.

Do not go, those eyes had said.

He didn't agree with all of her decisions in life, but he did know in the end that their people needed her. And she needed them perhaps even more.

None more so than her brother.

Rebekah had to ask once more. "Will you allow me to submit paperwork to have you admitted into a ward that treats your disease?"

Amos shook his head firmly. Rebekah sighed. "Susan likes to say that sunshine and nature are God's best medicines. I agree. So, will you consider going to a drier climate with lots of sunshine? Many people go to Arizona to treat the disease you have."

Amos didn't respond. That was a good sign. Rebekah would start filling out the paperwork tomorrow and leave it behind for Susan to finish. Provided Amos would allow it. Provided Susan survived.

CHAPTER 13

Light flamed right into Jimmy's eyeballs. It burned bad and he reached up to rub them. The pain subsided somewhat but his head still didn't feel quite right. Carefully shielding his eyes, Jimmy cracked them open to find a window on the other side of the room letting the sun shine right on his face. He blinked and looked around. Where was he?

A curtained wall like what was in doctor's offices stood to one side of the bed where he was stretched out. A blanket covered him to his chest and he looked under it to confirm his suspicion. Someone had stripped him down to his long johns.

Where was his six-gun?

Another look around the room showed his britches, shirt, and buckskin jacket folded neatly on a chair. His hat hung on one corner of the chair and his six-gun and belt hung from the other.

Jimmy kicked the blanket off with a grunt and swung his legs over the side of the bed to sit up. His head pounded, but it didn't feel nearly as bad as before he passed out.

How had he passed out and when?

He remembered the hotel lobby, the sheriff hauling away the

tail man, and the plump woman with her parasol. Had she hit him?

No. Jimmy must have just overdone it like Miss Rebekah warned him not to when she left. She was right. He still needed tending. But so did she.

That thought caused Jimmy to bolt to his feet. Where was Miss Rebekah now? Jimmy was supposed to meet her in Macy.

Jimmy staggered over to the chair, steadying himself on the back. He plopped his hat on and stuck his arms through his shirt sleeves, pulling it on in one motion. Britches on, he grabbed his boots, yanking one on. He tried to get the other on but it wouldn't go. He hopped and hopped and fell backward, right across the bed.

He stuck his foot straight up in the air, hooked his fingers in the boot straps and tugged hard. His foot was at the wrong angle and the boot refused to slip on.

"Good heavens, what are you doing?"

Jimmy wished it was the voice of the plump lady with the parasol. But no. That squeak belonged to the general store-keeper's daughter.

Jimmy rolled his head to the side to see her standing by the curtain wall, holding a tray of food. She looked odd at this angle, her pointy nose fierce and threatening. Didn't she have the decency to call out first, knowing he'd been in bed in his long johns?

Jimmy ignored her as he yanked on the boot that simply refused to cooperate.

With a huff, the girl plopped the tray on the now empty chair and turned to face him, arms crossed. "The doctor said you're supposed to stay in bed until tomorrow. You had a high fever and a gut wound he said wasn't done healing."

Jimmy rolled away from looking at her and pushed himself back up to a sitting position. He stood and stomped the stubborn boot into place, almost twisting his ankle in the process. He winced. "I've got a friend out there who needs me. How long have I been here anyway?"

"Two days."

Jimmy's eyes popped wide and he staggered around the girl to grab his gun belt and hat. "I gotta git."

"The only place you're going to get is back in that bed."

The girl reached out like she was going to grab him by the arm and sling him to the floor. Jimmy twisted to one side and scrambled over the bed to evade her.

"Nothin' doing."

He ran for the door, shrieks and insults flying after him.

CHAPTER 14

At the Omaha Agency boarding school at Macy, a flood of memories overcame Rebekah. That, combined with the fact that Charlie wouldn't travel to Sioux City to search for Jimmy, left her with little ability to concentrate on her patients. Thankfully, there were no serious cases among them, but it was still a long and tedious day for Rebekah. She was anxious to visit Susan, then get back to Sioux City and find out what happened to Jimmy.

Being in Macy made her uneasy. This was the first place Graham would look for her. But Amos had said the current Indian agent was away and no one would know she was there except the ones he wanted to know.

The school room where she had treated patients was suddenly empty. Or perhaps it had been that way for several minutes. Rebekah couldn't be certain as she seated herself at the teacher's desk to arrange her medical bag. She assessed what supplies she still had and what she would need to replenish before treating very many more.

Having Amos and his network bring patients to her was quite different from what she'd done the past three years in traveling the West. In a sense, this was more exhausting because the patients came one after another. Tremendously gratifying as well, if she allowed herself to stop worrying long enough to appreciate these precious days in her homeland.

A shadow fell across her bag and she looked up to see Amos there. She nodded at the bottles and bandages on the teacher's desk. "I'm low on almost everything. We will need to visit Susan's office to re-supply before I can treat anyone else."

Amos wasn't looking at her. Or the supplies. He was looking at her medical bag, worn from her most recent adventures. He touched it with two fingers, tracing the leather down the sides. Rebekah realized his other hand was behind his back. She rose from the chair, sensing he was preparing for a ceremonious moment. What that could be, she couldn't even venture a guess.

Amos met her eyes. There was indeed a look of ceremony in them.

"You have served our people well."

He brought his hand out from behind his back to reveal one of the most stunning sights Rebekah could imagine. He held a small medical bag, small enough to fit inside her regular one and sort her supplies more properly. The aspect that left her speechless was the fact that the entire bag was beaded.

Rebekah rocked back on her heels, mouth agape. She reached out and feathered her fingers across the cool glass beads. "How... Why..."

Amos held the bag higher and Rebekah realized she had delayed in accepting the gift. She took it carefully in both hands, turning it every which way to see the intricate patterns and fine bead work. This was what he had been working on while she was there? But no. There were too many hours in this beautiful and precious work of art. He must have started on it some time ago. He had been anticipating her return for some time. And he approved of it.

He approved of her. Approved of her chosen path in life, to walk in two worlds and to love and heal people in both.

Rebekah swallowed, a tear trailing down her cheek and dripping off.

She met Amos's eyes to see how they watered as well. His shoulders shook from a suppressed cough but Rebekah took a chance. She reached up and touched his cheek. He didn't move away.

"Thank you, my brother."

How she meant her simple appreciation for so much more than this beautiful bag.

The thunder of horse hooves broke the moment and Amos pulled back, going to the south window to look out. He said nothing, just strode for the door. Rebekah remained rooted in place. It was Charlie.

He and Amos exchanged a few brief words and her brother turned to her, his expression grim. She joined them, looking between the men.

Amos said, "Charlie went to Bancroft and saw someone he recognized."

Rebekah put a hand to her throat. Amos didn't need to speak the name. None of them did. She didn't want them to.

But she was the one who said it.

"Roger Graham."

CHAPTER 15

Rebekah absolutely, positively refused to leave the reservation without seeing her friend one last time. Who knew if it would truly be the last time she ever saw her?

Amos knew what to do. He led them on the westerly trail that angled south. Graham would follow the southern trail up to Macy, searching for Rebekah. By God's grace, they would miss him, see Susan at Bancroft, and Rebekah could catch the train back to Wyoming.

That left one problem. Where was Jimmy?

She would send a telegram from Bancroft to Jimmy in Sioux City. He had to still be there. Rebekah refused to think of him injured and stranded somewhere on the Winnebago or Omaha reservations.

Amos and Rebekah rode careful but hard to churn up the miles to Susan's place. They stopped in a ravine outside of Bancroft for Charlie to slip in. He discovered Graham had rented a buggy and left hours before.

When they arrived at the wood framed house, Rebekah

dismounted with her medical bag, the newly beaded bag tucked inside.

Rebekah rushed up the steps like she had the first time and didn't bother to knock as she let herself in and straight up the stairs.

Rosalie waited at the top for her, the door to Susan's room closed. Rebekah was nearly lost in the depths of her gaze. Was she too late to say goodbye?

Rosalie held out her hands as though she wanted to embrace Rebekah but didn't know how. Haltingly, Rosalie said, "Thank...you."

Rebekah touched the back of her hand and went to the door. She quietly opened it and stared.

Susan was sitting upright in bed, a flush of color on her dark-skinned cheeks. Her smile was radiant as she looked away from the man seated beside her. "Oh! Dear Rebekah. I've just had a report from Rosalie of each person you have helped in such a short time. You must tell me all about them and meet my husband..."

She faltered, her eyebrows drawing together.

No wonder. Rebekah was a positive mess from the hard ride and the thousand worries on her brow.

Susan extended her hand and Rebekah strode forward to grasp it. Susan's hands felt warm, and her color looked oh so much better! Perhaps Rebekah's coming had helped save her friend after all.

Susan asked, "What is wrong?"

Rebekah set her bag aside and seated herself on Susan's bed, taking her hand in both of hers. "Agent Graham was here in Bancroft. He is looking for me."

Susan bit her lip. "Then you must leave. Right away."

Leave.

Rebekah's gut wrenched. She clung to Susan's hand. How could she ever leave her people again after this return?

Rebekah closed her eyes. "How many more years must I endure?"

She felt Susan's hand softly stroking her hair. "Dearest. I remember as girls how we measured life in days and weeks and months. And now, we measure life in years. Someday, like our fathers, we will measure it by decades. Time is what it is and our God holds it in his hand just as He holds us."

Rebekah bent her head toward Susan's touch.

Strong hands wrapped around her shoulders and pulled her back. Amos knew she did not have the strength to part on her own.

A cry from downstairs had her jumping to her feet. She heard Rosalie shout from the bottom of the stairs as someone thundered up them at an incredible pace.

Rebekah gasped. There was nowhere to hide from Agent Graham. Amos stepped in front of her, body rigid. Then he relaxed and Rebekah recognized a precious voice shout, "Miss Rebekah!"

Amos stepped aside in time to keep from being leveled by Jimmy as he nearly tackled Rebekah in a hug. He backed up, face red from exertion and embarrassment.

"Sorry it took so long for me to get here. You all right, ma'am?"

His eyes were bloodshot and he had the look of a leftover fever that concerned Rebekah. But otherwise, he seemed none the worse for wear.

"I am well, Just Jimmy. Which is more than I can say for you. You need bedrest."

Jimmy shook his head vigorously. "No time, ma'am. As I was riding out of Macy, I heard someone greet this man by the name of Graham. We got trouble coming right behind me."

Rebekah swallowed and nodded. "I'm preparing to leave now. But before we do, I want you to meet someone very special."

The way Jimmy stood in awe and respect as he was introduced

to Doctor Susan La Flesche Picotte and her husband Henry made those extra moments of delay worth it.

But their time had run out and Rebekah forced herself to say her final goodbyes as Jimmy dragged her from the house, Amos following behind.

They mounted up, her and Jimmy, but Amos remained on the ground as he handed the reins to her. Rebekah suddenly realized this was goodbye between her and her brother, too.

Rebekah clutched the handle of her medical bag. She couldn't speak.

Amos did, resting his hand on her bag. "I will ask Doc Susan to write a letter for me to visit the place with dry air and sunshine."

Rebekah touched the back of his hand, then he lifted it in a farewell. Rebekah turned her horse to follow Jimmy out of Bancroft, forcing herself not to look back.

Darkness had a nasty and evil air about it on the Omaha Indian Reservation. Graham hated the place even before his wife and daughter died there.

Now the darkness wrapped its tentacles around his heart, his mind, his soul. But he would break free of it, once and for all when he had seen to destroying Rebekah LaRoche. The time had come.

At least, he had been convinced of that this morning when he arrived in Macy. Now, after traipsing across half the reservation well into the night, he was back in Bancroft near Susan La Flesche's home. He was irate, having the sinking suspicion that these Indians had done nothing but lead him on a wild goose chase for hours. From the first person he asked if there was an Indian doctor practicing medicine on the reservation, he had been given directions from one place to another and found that he had gone in a complete circle.

It felt like a conspiracy.

That was why Graham disregarded the last "lead" that he had been given and opted to cut through the circle and go straight to Susan La Flesche's house. He had no more respect for her as an

Indian woman doctor than he did Rebekah LaRoche. But he was certain an Indian woman had been treating patients all over the reservation the past few days. He was going to track her down and destroy her.

Graham was not welcome in Susan La Flesche's home, but her sister, who had foolishly left the reservation as many times as Susan, finally allowed him inside when he flashed the letter from the governor. She even led him upstairs when Susan called from her room for him to come up.

He found her in bed as though she were sick. That made him more angry.

"Have you been treating patients at a church, the boarding school, and a trading post the past few days?"

Susan La Flesche was a church going, self-proclaimed God-fearing Indian, and he would press into that to force the truth out of her. To force her to be a witness that Rebekah LaRoche had been practicing medicine on the reservation.

Susan La Flesche looked alarmed. "Are my patients unwell?"

Graham ground his teeth together, relishing the pain. "I want you to tell me the truth right now. Is Rebekah LaRoche on the reservation?"

Susan La Flesche looked at him, innocent as a newborn babe. "No. She is not."

Graham whipped the governor's letter from his pocket, ripped it to shreds, and left.

It was not over between him and Rebekah LaRoche. He would have his vengeance—and his peace—someday.

CHAPTER 17

Rebekah hardly knew how to walk up the path to the McKinnon Ranch house as Jimmy stayed by the buggy. Doctor McKinnon stood there on the porch, hands in his pockets as he watched her approach.

Laramie was no where in sight, which she appreciated. After discovering Susan's recent marriage, she was not prepared to face him. Doctor McKinnon was enough for this moment.

She felt shattered and pieced back together. Now, seeing her uncle, she felt shattered again.

She made it to the top of the steps and set her medical bag in one of the rocking chairs to face her uncle. His mouth was pulled tight. She waited for him to speak first.

"I didn't know if you would return."

His voice rooted her in the realization that she was who she was, no matter where she was. Her heart would always belong with her people and she would never stop trying to return to them. But this was home too, home with this dear man who loved her like a daughter.

"I thought you might have another mission for me."

He nodded stiffly and Rebekah recognized his attempt to hold back his emotions. "I do. If you are up for the challenge."

It was Rebekah's turn to nod stiffly before Uncle Robert opened his arms to her and she melted into them.

How could she have willingly caused him so much pain? How could she ever say how sorry she was that she had?

Doctor McKinnon whispered into her hair, "I'm glad you went. Selfish old man that I am, I'm gladder you came back."

He released her and Rebekah took a shuddering breath, trying to lighten her soul of its heaviness. How different her white uncle's culture was to her people. She had missed it, just as she missed her people when she was away. She belonged in both those worlds.

The lone buffalo standing against the wind.

She braved a smile. "Now, where is this new mission you have for me?"

Doctor McKinnon's grimace was sincere. "The United States Penitentiary. Leavenworth."

Rebekah raised her eyebrows but said nothing. It sounded like an easier mission than what she had just been through.

"Let me freshen up and you can tell me all about it."

Doctor McKinnon retrieved her medical bag. "And you can tell me all about your return to the reservation. I'm sure it was quite an experience."

How right her uncle was.

Dearest reader,

Thank you for reading *The Return (Doc Beck Westerns Book 9)*. I truly hope it entertained and delighted you!

If you fell in love with the main characters, Rebekah, aka "Doc Beck," and Jimmy, you'll be excited to know there are more books to come!

While you're waiting, I'd be thrilled if you took a moment to write your thoughts in the form of a review for *The Return* and post it on your favorite retail outlet and Goodreads. You'll help other readers find this series.

To discover more of my books, free short stories, and to generally stay in touch with me, I invite you to join my VIP reader newsletter. You'll receive a free copy of *The Executions*, book one in my *Choctaw Tribune* Historical Fiction series. Please join me through: bit.ly/ChoctawTribune.

Speaking of history, the character of Doc Beck was inspired by Dr. Susan La Flesche (Omaha), who is hailed as the first American Indian to earn a medical degree. In continued research, my mother found Dr. Isabel Cobb (Cherokee), the first woman physician in Indian Territory, in very nearly the same years as Dr. La Flesche.

Lastly, if you're not familiar with my heritage books based on my Choctaw history and culture, you can check them out on www.SarahElisabethWrites.com.

Questions? Send them my way: me@sarahelisabethwrites.com

—Sarah Elisabeth Sawyer
Historical Fiction and Western author
Tribal member of the Choctaw Nation of Oklahoma

ABOUT THE AUTHOR

SARAH ELISABETH SAWYER is a story archaeologist. She digs up shards of past lives, hopes, and truths, and pieces them together for readers today. The Smithsonian's National Museum of the American Indian honored her as a literary artist through their Artist Leadership Program for her work in preserving Choctaw Trail of Tears stories. She is the creator of the Fiction Writing: American Indians digital course. (FictionCourses.com)

A tribal member of the Choctaw Nation of Oklahoma, she writes historical fiction from her hometown in Texas, partnering with her mother, Lynda Kay Sawyer, in continued research for future works. Learn more at SarahElisabethWrites.com, Choctaw Spirit.com, and Facebook.com/SarahElisabethSawyer.